Most Dangerous

Kevin L. Williams

Published by KLW Publishing, 2023.

Chapter 1

Zeke Kinney had the dream again. Running through the woods. Searching...hunting...looking for prey. The same dream which had intruded into his mind night after night for a week straight. Sometimes he hunted deer and elk, other times sheep or cattle that wandered away from their flock or herd. Zeke even dreamed about the old brown grizzly with the thick paws, heavy hide, and long teeth. The bear called Scar. The one who had stalked these woods for more than a decade. Scar was ancient and not afraid of anything on this earth.

Zeke had a run in with Scar when he was around thirteen. He was out hiking. Tom told him to stay close to home due to sightings by hunters where they claimed the old bear was aggressive. But of course, Zeke didn't mind. Zeke, like lots of young men his age, thought he knew best. Zeke wished he would see that old bear so he could look him in the eyes and show him who the boss was. So, filled with piss and vinegar, Zeke marched out onto Pine Ridge, armed with a pellet gun and pride.

Zeke climbed the rock formations he knew, found an old spruce to lean against, and he waited. And waited. And waited. Zeke waited until long shadows crept over the land and he nodded off. When thirteen-year-old Zeke woke up he found himself face to face with fourteen hundred pounds of pissed off bear. Old Scar was angry that this interloper had the nerve to invade his territory. Zeke had no escape. He sat back against the tree and waited to die...that is...until old Scar did something Zeke would never forget. The bear leaned in, sniffed Zeke's face and neck, then backed off with a grunt.

Zeke was terrified and humiliated. But, he remembered how the bear had looked into his eyes...No...into his *SOUL*. It was as if they were kindred spirits. But this time Zeke's dream was not about old Scar, it was about the strange man. The one who looked at children on the street in a way that made Zeke's skin crawl. He was the prey tonight.

Zeke rounded a tall fir tree and stopped just south of the clearing he had known since he was a young boy. Zeke knew this land like his own body. Every shallow ridge. Every valley. All the culverts and best places to cross the river. Zeke knew where to find the best ridge to sit on during the afternoon sun, and the cool shady spots during the peak of summer. Zeke knew all this and more. He caressed the trunk of the fir, gliding his hand over the initials *Z.K.* carved into it more than a decade ago.

Zeke knew something else too. He knew that *Johnny Gamble*, the man who liked children, had someone with him in the truck. A boy of ten.

And this Zeke would not tolerate.

As Zeke watched from his side of the clearing all he could make out in the semi-darkness was the outline of the truck, the black paint blending into the rest of the forest. Zeke tried his other senses. He sniffed the night air. It brought back a dozen smells and aromas. A sound reached his ears as he stood there. Crying. Zeke crept from the cover of the trees and stalked closer to the truck. He saw the man pull the boy from the truck and drag him through the tree line where they moved from his field of vision. Zeke's hands shook. The rage started to overtake him.

It was time.

As if answering a siren call that went unheard, the Moon, low and full, crept from behind a bank of clouds. It was the new moon beginning the first night of its three-day cycle. Zeke looked up and felt its power.

Felt its pull.

Felt it calling to him...

Zeke crouched down and focused on the prey. He ran past the truck. The woods flying by him as he increased speed. Zeke veered into the woods at the spot where the man took his captive. He spotted them about fifteen yards away. Zeke let instinct take over and he jumped at the man, smashing into him with the force of a small car. They tumbled to the grass, rolled several more feet, landing at the base of a tree. Zeke stood over the man. He could tell that the impact had resulted in a broken back. Zeke stared down at the strange man who liked children and smelled the fear pouring off him in waves.

"No...please...don't..."

Zeke hesitated. He glanced over his shoulder at the traumatized boy huddled on the ground too terrified to move. Zeke looked at the prey again.

"Please..."

Zeke raised his face to the heavens, letting out a horrific scream of rage. Then, he savaged the prey, enjoying every minute of it.

Zeke bolted upright from his bed. Sweat soaked the bedsheet and dripped from his face. Zeke swung his legs off the bed, stared down and realized his fists were clenched. Zeke opened them and inhaled. His palms were bloody. Deep gouges lined them. Zeke inspected his fingertips. They were bloody also. Zeke stood and stumbled over to his tiny bathroom. He turned the cold water on and let it splash over his torn hands.

Sunlight peppered the small window over his bed, alerting him to the beginning of his work day. He bandaged his hands and walked back into his bedroom to change. Zeke stretched his muscular frame as he passed the cracked mirror next to the closet. Zeke was in fantastic shape. He had the frame of a bodybuilder, but he had never spent one day inside a gym. Zeke's physique had been forged in the fires of hard manual labor.

Working on his father's property cutting wood, hauling farm equipment around, digging fences, and doing odd jobs for the folks in Tarton's Mill.

This was the small town a few miles south of Zeke's cabin. It was located in the western portion of Minnesota, but due to some zoning chicanery years ago, it had been scrubbed off the official maps. For most people in the country and the state, Tarton's Mill did not exist...and the people of Tarton's Mill liked this just fine.

Tarton's Mill was a small town like other small towns across the country. It had one main street (called Main Street) that divided the town, traveling north and south. Shops and small businesses lined Main Street. A bakery, pharmacy, grocery store, diner. Three bars that competed for customers on the weekdays. A video store hanging on by a thread in this digital age, and a washeteria where washers and dryers still cost .50, and an old woman named May Ellen folded them for $1 a load. At the far end of Main Street there was a bed and breakfast and a gas station. Beyond that, the open road beckoned.

Zeke loved this town, even if he was treated like an outsider at times. This didn't really bother him though. All he cared about was that the town residents treated his dad well. And they did. Everyone in Tarton's Mill loved Tom Kinney. He was the local pharmacist and had lived in the Mill, as it was known, all his life except during his military service stateside in California for a few years before deploying to Vietnam. To some, Tom was the heartbeat of the Mill. Everyone came and went through Tom's pharmacy, so he was included in all the gossip, activities, events, and goings on. Tom knew all the wonderful secrets, and the secrets that needed to remain behind closed doors. Still, Tom was a private man. Even though he knew the Mill's secrets, no one except Zeke knew his. And even Zeke didn't know them all.

Zeke touched four old scars that crisscrossed his chest. They were faded and healed, but still visible. Zeke started to reach into the closet. Something made him glance over at his bedside clock. It was 8:00 am.

"Damn."

Zeke decided to skip the shower for now and got dressed.

Tom Atkins checked his watch, drank some coffee from his Marine Corps coffee mug, and checked his watch again.

"That boy." He chuckled to himself with a smile.

Tom sipped more coffee and walked to the back of the store. On the whole, his pharmacy resembled a general store more than a modern pharmacy. There was a long, old fashioned counter along the right side where he doled out ice cream sodas for the kids on Saturdays. Maybe eight or ten shelves filled the main area in the store, stocked with enough to keep up with small town demand. But, without a substantial storage room to hold more, Tom had to make frequent trips to Cold Water over forty miles away to restock and pick up specialty meds from time to time. Past the shelves was the actual pharmacist counter.

Behind this a small office where Tom paid bills and talked to the even smaller roster of doctors listed in his rolodex. Tom often thought maybe he should keep those contacts in his cell phone, but that was a young person's game. Zeke made him start texting six months ago and that was as far as Tom was willing to go. He did have a laptop computer to work on that was okay, but most of this work was done by Lila, his part-time assistant who also pulled shifts as a waitress at the diner. Maybe he would ask Lila to transfer the contacts from the rolodex to his cell. Lord knows he could not figure it out.

Lila was a good girl. She was an orphan, raised by her great aunt Sylvia who ran the bed and breakfast at the other end of town. Tom liked Lila because she had a certain honesty about her. She was unguarded in a way most folks in the Mill weren't. Lila said what she thought no matter what. She also had a strange way of knowing what folks were feeling if she touched them. Lila claimed she had the *"second sight"*, which was some kind of gypsy thing Tom suspected since she always referred to her people as being gypsies. Tom wasn't sure if it was true or not, but Lila believed it and that was enough for Tom.

Either way, all that mattered to Tom was that she was a lovely young lady and she was sweet on his boy. Lila had taken a liking to Zeke the first time she saw Zeke after he came back to the Mill. And Zeke liked her too, although the boy was too damned shy to do anything about it. Tom might have to rectify that at some point. He didn't want Zeke growing old like Tom and living alone. He wanted more for his son like all parents do. Tom wanted Zeke to live a full life, get married, maybe have some babies.

Tom choked up at this thought. Could Zeke have children? Would he ever have a life like that? Tom hoped so. But hoping and reality do not always mix.

What about...?

No! Stop it Tom Kinney! You and Zeke will figure it out. Like always. Get it together Marine!

Well, that was a bridge he and Zeke would cross together, but not now. He still had time before opening the store at ten. He had some accounting to get done and more coffee to drink. Tom appraised his coffee mug. The Marines had been good to him and Valerie. Twenty years in the Corps and she never complained. Not once. Sure, he had seen many horrible things during the War, but it never made him change his outlook on life. Well, Valerie had helped with that. She had been the eternal optimist.

Never forget Tom...we ALWAYS have hope. Right?

Yes darling. You're right.

And, that is why you are a good husband...because you know I'm always right!

Tom smiled at his late wife's words. When he squinted he could just make out the outlines of her face in the golden rays of sunset when he sat in the worn rocker on the porch. Tom sensed her presence inside when he started a fire in the winter, or when he sat at their kitchen table with the big bay windows, facing the edge of their property. When he stared out into the distance he imagined her looking back at him from Heaven. And this thought was good. Yes, Tom had lived a good life even though his Valerie was gone.

Chapter 2

Zeke pushed his old truck as fast as he dared on the slippery backroads leading into the Mill. It fishtailed and threatened to jump off the road a few times, but Zeke manhandled it with ease. He was used to speeding on these roads. From seventeen until now, except for the *dark time*, he raced them.

Always pushing the limits of the truck and himself.

"Damn, damn, damn. I should've set the alarm. Pops is gonna be pissed."

Zeke gunned the truck, trying to milk every ounce of juice from the carburetor. He smiled as he crested the slope leading down into the Mill and...KA-THUNK!

"Shit!"

The truck shuddered and quit. Zeke placed it into neutral and coasted along the road, hoping to use the momentum to restart the truck. He turned the engine off and on, slipped the clutch, and slammed the gear shift into first. Nothing doing. The truck coughed out thick black smoke and shut off.

Zeke maneuvered the truck to the side of the road, parking it along Mr. Haverty's fence-line, and climbed out. *Two more miles to the Mill...half a mile to the pharmacy...I should be there in no time.* Zeke grabbed his backpack from the bed of the deceased truck and sprinted toward the Mill.

Zeke walked in the door of the pharmacy just as Tom was walking from the back wearing his trademark, white pharmacy coat with the shortened sleeves. Tom wrinkled his nose up.

"Cutting it a little close eh son?"

Zeke smiled at his father. "Why do you insist on wearing the one with the short sleeves? It's goofy." Zeke said, a smile playing on his lips.

"You're one to talk. Coming in here looking like a dust bunny. Did you run? You smell like sweat."

Zeke nodded as he walked his backpack to the office, placed it on one of the chairs, and came back out.

"Truck died up on the slope by Mr. Haverty's."

Tom eyed his son. "How long ago?"

Zeke was rummaging through the cooler behind the soda fountain counter.

"Ah...about ten minutes I guess."

Tom walked over and stared at his son. "You ran two and half miles in ten minutes? Zeke, that's just doesn't sound right son."

Zeke fished out a water and shrugged off any thought of the run as if it was nothing. But, to Tom it was something. A something he worried about and fussed over. A something that might become a real BIG something if they weren't careful. They had to be careful. Out here, away from most other folks, their secret was safe. But...

Tom noticed the bandages on Zeke's hands. He came over to inspect them.

"What happened?"

"Guess I had a bad dream. Ripped them up a little. It's no biggie." Zeke said.

"Let me check it out. Come on." Tom walked Zeke back to the counter and pulled out some bandages and antiseptic wipes. They sat in the two chairs behind the counter and Tom unwrapped the bandages as careful as he could. The bandages were bloody. When Tom stripped them off he examined Zeke's hands. Tom frowned.

"What's wrong Pops?"

Tom stared at his son's hands. Turned them over.

"When did this happen?" Tom asked.

"Last night. Well, I noticed them this morning."

"Uh...they're healed." Tom sat back and scratched his head.

Zeke looked at his hands. The flesh on his palms was raw and inflamed, but there were no gouges. His hands were in fact healed.

"Wait. No. They were all ripped up. My fingers too. Like I dug them in. I don't understand." Zeke said. A shadow of something unseen passed between the two men. They understood that this was important. It signaled a shift that neither was willing to talk about. Not yet.

"You're healing faster now. Used to take twice as long." Tom stood. "We need to call someone. A specialist maybe."

Zeke stood. "And tell them what? That I'm some kind of freak? So they can test my blood and put me in a cage? No! That is never gonna happen! Not again!" Zeke paced the room like a caged animal. Tom stepped over and placed a hand on Zeke's shoulder.

"Son, I'm not saying we need to go that far. What I am saying is that we might be past the time where we can go it alone. We need help son."

Zeke stared at his father. HIS protector. His rock. He loved this man with a ferocity that clouded everything else in the world out. Zeke needed his father. He was the only one who understood.

"Sorry Pops. It's just that..."

"I know son. I know. Those were dark times, but we've moved on. And we need to keep moving on. But, we still need to figure out some kind of game plan."

Tom pushed the thought away. A sound like looming thunder shook the front windows of the pharmacy. Tom walked from behind the counter and over to the front windows. He knew the sound was coming from the end of Main Street. And, it kept increasing. The rumble becoming more ominous. Zeke joined Tom at the window.

"What's that? Construction equipment?" Zeke asked.

"Nope. Motorcycles. Lots of 'em." Tom answered.

Tom and Zeke saw the source of the thunder. Tom was right. It was a large group of people riding motorcycles. Thirty, perhaps forty of them. Even in the cool air which signaled the first signs of winter some of the riders were dressed for much warmer weather. They were a motley crew. Some dressed like 1% motorcycle clubs dress: Sleeveless leather vests, worn jeans, white or black t-shirts, tall cowboy boots, or sturdy black, steel-toed ones worn from the constant action of changing gears on the left side, and braking on the right. Baseball caps turned backward or bandanas adorned their heads. A few wore helmets. The majority did not.

The rest of the group looked as if they drifted straight out of some post-apocalyptic roadshow. Tom tried to remember the name of the movie with the drifter who helped a bunch of folks escape some marauders. Damn if he could remember much these days, Tom thought as the group roared up Main Street, past the pharmacy, and stopped at the diner two blocks up.

"This can't be good Pops." Zeke said. He was restless. Tom could feel anxious energy flowing off him.

"Let's not get ahead of ourselves. Folks are probably passing through. We're the only other stop for the next one hundred and twelve miles if you're going north you know." Tom said.

"I know Pops, but something just feels off. I can't say what. It just does."

Zeke started for the door.

"I'm going to check on Lila."

"Okay. Just remember to grab that load from Dale on the way back. We need to stack 'em by the back door until I can get 'em all sorted out. Okay son?"

"No problem. See you in a few." Zeke didn't turn his head to look at Tom. His focus was down the street where the bikers were backing up along the curbs on either side of Main Street. The few folks out this early gave the newcomers a wide berth, coupled with furtive over-the-shoulder glances. Tom watched Zeke stroll down the street. That's one of the many things he loved about his son. He was very protective.

Chapter 3

The bikers flooded the diner. Zeke picked his pace up, but was interrupted by an older woman named Mrs. Ellis. She stopped him with a wave of her chubby little arm. She was dressed in bag shaped skirt, thick coat too warm for the not-quite-cold weather, and a silly hat that flopped from side to side as she made her way towards him.

"Young man! Young man!"

Zeke slowed his pace and put on his best smile. Mrs. Ellis leaned against him, using his arm as a support pillar. Zeke smiled at her. He wanted to run to the diner and see if Lila was okay, but Mrs. Ellis had always been nice to him and his dad, so he didn't want to appear rude.

"Zeke...would you...whew! I am so out of breath from running to catch up with you!" She sucked in several huge gulps of air before finishing. "Your lovely father said you could help me move that old ice-box off my back porch and take it to the dump. Can you do that for me? I don't have a lot of money to pay you, but I can pay you something for your time of course! I can even cook you dinner. Oh! Better yet, I can cook dinner for you and that handsome father of yours! What do you say?"

Zeke watched the bikers jostling for position as they surged into the diner like a pack of wild animals.

"Yes ma'am, I can help you no problem. I just need to eat some breakfast first. I can come by your place around noon if that works for you."

"Perfect!" Mrs. Ellis said as she clapped her hands. "I'll see you later!" She started off across the street, stopped and leaned into Zeke. She lowered her voice to a whisper, which didn't make any sense because there was no one else around.

"Did you hear about the body?"

"What body?" Zeke asked.

"Marge Patterson said that Ellen Williams told Genie Tubbs that Old Johnny Gamble was killed last night!"

"Who's Johnny Gamble?" Zeke bounced the name around in his head. It sounded familiar, but he couldn't quite place it.

"Oh, everybody knows who Johnny Gamble is!" She leaned closer to his ear. "I'm not one to gossip, but they said he liked the boys if you know what I mean!"

Zeke wanted to be anywhere but here right now. He didn't care if someone was gay or straight. To each his own, that's what Pops always said. And Zeke agreed with him. Zeke angled past Mrs. Ellis, hoping his body language made it clear that he needed to leave. It didn't. Mrs. Ellis kept rambling.

"I'm sure I don't know what you mean ma'am." Zeke said.

"No...I don't mean *gay*. I mean...he liked the *BOYS*." She shuddered as she said it. "The county sheriff found his body this morning near Pine Bluff Road. The scuttlebutt is some kind of wolf tore him up! Just awful! I mean, he was a despicable man and all. Lots of rumors about holing up with little boys or something. But, to be eaten alive! Just horrible! But, of course this is all gossip, and I'm not one to gossip of course! I suppose the man had it coming to him. Karmic destiny...Okay then! Toodles! See you at noon!"

Mrs. Ellis skipped away, leaving Zeke to ponder what she just said.

... eaten alive...

Zeke shuddered at the thought and hurried to the diner.

Lila Clark was sick of serving customers. Its not that she hated customers, hell, she knew all of them anyway. Every day and night the same folks came and went. They ordered the same eggs, biscuits, ham, gravy, toast, and coffee as every other morning. In the afternoon it was burgers, sandwiches, soup, grilled cheese. For dinner, classic staples like walleye, tater tot hot dish, lutefisk, and of course, grain belt beer.

Day after day, it was always the same. She loved the customers and their stories and gossip, but she wanted more. Lila wanted to go somewhere exciting. To do something exciting. When she looked at the waitresses she worked with Lila felt the shawl of old age descending. They were wonderful women, but Lila felt their despair. She felt the loneliness and acceptance of the plainness of their lives. It's not that they were sad, but just...Lila knew these women had given up on their hopes and dreams the moment they began working at the diner, and this is something that Lila did not want.

Lila was from a long line of women who had the *second sight* as her Nana had told her. Since Birth Lila had been able to perceive how others felt by either touching them, or just being near them. When Lila was younger she thought having the sight was a curse. Other kids made fun of her, calling her Spooky Lila. She endured nonstop taunting until the age of seventeen, when Sheila Bennet, her high school nemesis, grabbed her by the ponytail to show some other kids how weak she thought Lila was.

Lila touched Sheila on the face, and for the first time in her life, she *pushed* the sight, instead of *pulling* it, causing Sheila to feel all the pain and heart ache Lila had endured for years and years. Sheila fell to the ground and started crying. She was overwhelmed by the emotions Lila had made her open to, and was unable to handle it. The incident shook Sheila up, but didn't cause her any permanent damage.

But, she understood that Lila was not the person to tease.

Lila never told anyone about what happened, but the teasing and abuse stopped. Lila heard from former schoolmates that Sheila had some memory issues now or something. Lila felt bad about it, but a person had a right to defend themselves. Now that Lila was an adult she understood that her second sight was a gift and not a curse. She was given this gift to benefit others. Lila just had to figure out how to share it, and with whom.

When the biker group entered the diner, Lila felt their deadly energy. Malice and danger dripped off them like summer rain. She had seen lots of bikers come through from time to time, and they were always nice, well-mannered, and fun-loving folks. These people here were not. Her regulars felt it too. This time of day the customers were older, retired folks who ate at the diner as part of their daily routine. Now, the peace had been shattered by the arrival of this motley crew. They slithered and squeezed into every seat in the diner. The sound level went up as they cursed, laughed, and made an all-around ruckus. The fact that they were disturbing her regular customers pissed Lila off. She took a deep breath and walked over.

Chapter 4

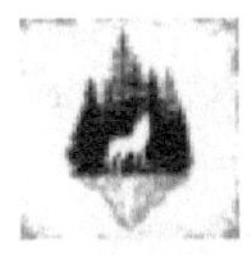

ALEXANDRIA, VIRGINIA - BLACK SITE: 12:20am

Two people huddled around the small metal desk inside this plain one-story house. From the outside, it appeared as if a family of three owned it. It had a steep driveway in the front, small garden near the porch, and one large tree overlooking the cracked sidewalk out front. In back, there was an alley which ran the length of the block, passing all eight houses. All in all, the house was unremarkable. Hammad Ajobai and Steph Woods conferred together over a large map. They were dressed in black tactical gear. Their weapons, Sig Saur handguns and H&K machine guns, were laid out on a table against one wall.

Inside, the house was utilitarian and not a living space at all. There was no furniture, the walls were bare and white. The only signs of habitation were a small refrigerator and microwave in the kitchen. Paper plates, utensils, and plastic cups for brief meals, and one working bathroom. The third occupant of the house, Loren Tepps, Team Leader, sat on the edge of the tub in the bathroom. She was also dressed like the men in all black tactical clothing and black boots. Her pants were around her ankles. She stared down at her inner thigh. On it were several scars from repeated knife cuts on her thigh. Loren stared at the cuts as if reading tea leaves. Loren studied the cuts, investigated them, tried to divine meaning from them. She drew her tactical knife from the scabbard on her hip, placed the blade against her thigh and made a shallow cut. Blood welled up and Loren tamped it down with a washcloth. Cutting didn't even hurt anymore. She was deadened to the pain. Immune to it.

She embraced the pain like a lover. Loren poised the knife for a second cut when someone knocked on the door.

"Hey Boss. You alright? We got the mission brief in three."

Loren lowered the knife. Dabbed her thigh once more, stood and buckled her pants. She went to the sink, washed the knife off.

"Be right out." Loren said. Her voice sounded robotic to her own ears, but she was positive that she sounded normal and gruff to her team.

"Roger that." The voice seemed to accept what she said at face value. Good. Loren had to keep up her stamina and energy. Keep up appearances. Loren liked Hammad. He was solid. Her number one. Reliable, loyal, courageous, and skilled. He would make a great replacement when she was gone. Steph too. Best tracker she had ever worked with. Together they made one helluva team.

She stared at her reflection. Loren was not old, but not young either. At forty-seven, maybe too old to still lead missions in the field. Most of her contemporaries were holding down office positions, or going about the business of having families, raising children. She and Frank never had children. It was their choice at the time. If she'd only known how little time they had together. Would she have chosen different? Perhaps. Perhaps not.

She stared at the strands of grey visible throughout her blond highlights. She should get that colored. But why? Frank was dead so what did her appearance matter? She wasn't interested in dating or any of that nonsense.

Loren had ONE focus in her life: *The Mission*.

It was everything. It was ALL to her. Nothing else mattered. And, when it came down to it, everyone was expendable. Hammad. Steph. The Bosses back at ODESSA. Everyone. All Loren cared about was finding the target and terminating with extreme prejudice. At any cost. All other priorities were negligible in her mind.

Of course, Loren was the only one who knew this, and it would stay this way. Loren stared into the mirror once more.

Stay focused. Almost game time.

Loren left the bathroom, joined Hammad and Steph at the table. Hammad held up a GPS tracker device. It was about the size of a tablet device, but bulkier. He shared the screen with them.

"Last sighting was here. Denver trail's cold though. No sightings or activity for months."

"Nothing from local traffic?" Loren asked.

Steph interjected. "Not so far. We followed up a few things but they were your typical bear or mountain lion sightings...occasional wolf."

"Our guy didn't just disappear into smoke. He's hiding out in a community somewhere that he can blend in. Not bring too much attention to himself." Loren said.

"He'll surface. It's just a matter of time. One traumatic trigger and...BAM!" Steph said with a snap of his fingers.

"I agree. Sooner or later. Then he's ours." Loren said.

The men nodded their heads in agreement. Hammad went through a few other details. Loren listened, but a portion of her brain was focused on the hunt ahead. She knew the target was out there. Walking around in broad daylight. Living carefree. It wasn't fair, but soon she would settle that debt. Yes.

Soon.

Chapter 5

Lila whispered to her frightened co-workers that she would take the orders. She walked over and zeroed in on the man she thought was the leader.

Caution Lila! Be strong, but respectful.

"Morning! What can I do for you fine folks today? Breakfast I assume?" Lila asked.

The leader looked up from his menu. He was a striking man in his mid-fifties. Much better dressed than his compatriots. Mathias Pilgrim stared up at Lila. He smiled. This smile disarmed many because it was a nice smile. It made Mathias seem like a decent guy. But, decent was far from Mathias. His time as a career convict and criminal had left a malice in Mathias' heart that Lila could see. She sensed a bright red aura of hate hovering over him, so strong it stung her. Every one of her instincts told her to run from this man. She forced the feelings down.

"Ma'am! I and my entourage wish to be served...post-haste! Sit down you rabble and show the good folks of Tarton's Mill some respect." Mathias said. He waved his hand with a flourish, as if he was on stage quoting Shakespeare. Lila left the smile on her face.

"Sure thing. If you can restrain these animals long enough for me to take their orders I'd appreciate it."

Mathias stared at her, and for a moment Lila wasn't sure if he was going to beat her or kiss her. Mathias smiled.

"Oh, I like our moxy fair maiden! Yes of course! Lads and ladies. Tell the young lady your meal requests, and be NICE!"

Zeke walked in as Lila took their orders. They caught each other's eye and smiled. Zeke nestled himself into a small booth toward the back where he could watch the rowdy group. He stared at Mathias and figured him for the leader due to the deference everyone showed him. When he laughed or made a joke they all laughed.

Betty, an older waitress served Zeke coffee. She smiled and walked off, but Zeke could tell she was nervous. He glanced at the other customers. They stared into their plates or coffee as if discovering new life forms. He watched Lila as she took orders.

God. She's beautiful.

Zeke thought Lila was the prettiest girl he'd ever seen. She had shoulder length brown hair. Well, sometimes it was blonde, or purple, or red depending on her mood, but it was a nice cut. She was curvy, with nice round hips, full breasts, and lovely calves. He was so glad Lila wasn't built like some of those Hollywood girls with big breasts and skinny legs. That was not attractive to him one bit. Zeke saw photographs in an art book one time at school that reminded him of Lila. *Rubenesque* he thought the term was, or something like that. Regardless, she was lovely. Zeke could've spent the entire day watching her, but that would come off as creepy he thought.

After Lila gave the orders to the cook she walked over.

"Hey Zeke."

"Hi Lila."

"Ham and eggs again?" She asked.

"I need my protein." Zeke said with a smile.

"Do you ever eat anything else?"

He grinned. "Eggs and ham."

"Alright smarty-pants. Ham and eggs it is! To go?"

"Please. I have some jobs to take care of."

Lila stared at Zeke. Concern in her eyes.

"Haven't seen you in awhile. Still doing odd jobs?"

"Yeah. Whatever pays." Zeke said.

"Why don't you work at the pharmacy with your dad?"

Zeke laughed. "I do some stuff for him. Picking up and making deliveries and such. But, honestly, that is WAY too much together time for us! We are too much alike. Besides, I've always been better with my hands. I like making things."

"Yeah. Makes sense." She started to walk away. "Hey. Did you hear about the pedophile that was killed last night? Heard he was gutted...some kind of animal did it. I'm betting it was that old bear. Pretty terrible huh?"

Zeke was rocked by her statement. All the color drained from his face as a furious stream of images flashed through his mind:

Zeke stood over the man who liked children.
Zeke smelled the fear pouring off him in waves.

"No...please...don't..."
Blood...
Screaming...
Howling...
"Zeke? Zeke? You okay? Lila's voice sounded far away...

Zeke glanced up and saw her watching him. "You okay Zeke? Catching a cold?"

"Uh...no. I don't get sick...much."

"Well, I better get your food so you don't pass out on me!"

Zeke recovered enough to ask her something.

"Hey...um...I heard that the new Science Fiction movie is playing in the next town...thought maybe you might want...I don't know...maybe..."

Lila smiled. "I'd love to go with you. If that's what you're asking Zeke. You asking me out on a date?"

Zeke was flustered. "Yeah."

"Let me know the date and time." She wrote her number on her small order pad, tore it off and handed it to him.

"Keep in touch."

Lila walked past Mathias' group on her way to check out their orders. Mathias' number two man, Blackie, grabbed hold of Lila's wrist as she passed. Blackie was a rough looking man in his forties. Muscular, with scars adorning his face and neck, rewards from years of knife fights and brawling in low level Mixed Martial Arts venues. He was bald and the top of his head had a grinning Reaper Skull tattoo.

"Hey…don't bring us any cold coffee. You better brew a fresh pot for us." Blackie said.

Zeke saw this. His lips pulled back in a snarl. Underneath the table Zeke's hand convulsed. Lila smiled at Blackie and kept walking. Blackie smacked her on the butt before she was out of reach and laughed to his buddies.

Zeke pushed his chair back so hard it crashed to the ground. He walked over to Blackie and stared down at him.

"Apologize…now."

Blackie stared at Zeke. He stood and smiled.

"You best be on your way son. The only thing on today's menu for you is pain." Blackie said.

Zeke continued staring at Blackie. Everyone in the diner held their breath. Some of the group stood up and took positions around Zeke. Mathias seemed amused as he watched these two Alpha Males square off.

"Apologize to her. Last time I ask." Zeke said.

Blackie didn't answer. He pulled a knife out and up to slash Zeke on the face. Zeke caught Blackie's arm mid-air and held it in an iron grip. It was as if Blackie's arm ran into a wall. Zeke squeezed causing Blackie's eyeballs to bulge out of his head. Blackie dropped the knife. Mathias' men didn't know what to do. They were shocked because Blackie was the strongest man they knew. Everyone feared and respected his ferocity and strength. Zeke squeezed harder until pain-tears sprouted from Blackie's eyes. He glanced over at Lila.

"I'm…I'm sorry Ma'am…" Blackie grunted.

Lila gave a little nod. "Thank you."

Zeke pulled Blackie close to his face and whispered in his ear.

"Don't you ever speak to her or touch her again. EVER." Zeke let go and walked over to the counter. Lila smiled and handed Zeke his order.

"Here's your order Zeke. Come back and see me?" Their fingers connected as she handed him the bag of food. Zeke smiled back. He stared over at Mathias and his group, his eyes stopping on Blackie. Zeke frowned and backed out of the diner.

The tension seemed to evaporate as soon as Zeke left. The group was quiet now, all their bluster gone. Blackie cradled his forearm and stared at his plate, unable to make eye contact with anyone. Mathias sat back and drank some coffee. He grinned.

"Now who was that?" Mathias asked no one in particular.

The minute Zeke stumbled from the diner the convulsions hit him. Wave after wave of pain, surging throughout his body. He fell against the building wall, but kept moving. He turned into the small alley between buildings, made it a few feet in so he was away from view of the street, and collapsed near the dumpsters. He grimaced as another wave hit him.

"No...not here..." Zeke breathed in and out in great, ragged gasps. The sound, guttural...feral. He closed his eyes, fighting against some strange and horrible impulse. The world went silent. Then, Zeke heard a roaring noise. He smelled the woods and tall grasses laid over with early winter frost.

Then...another sound.

Shallow.

Distant.

He *knew* this sound.

It was closer. Insistent.

TOM. His father calling to him.

"Zeke..."

Zeke knew Tom was close, but he couldn't focus. The roaring noise in his ears and convulsions in his body fought for Zeke's attention. Zeke felt loving hands embrace him. His first instinct was to fight, but the hands were strong and steady. As the hands held Zeke fast, a calm voice broke through the chaos in Zeke's mind and body. A steady drumbeat. Over and over...

"Zeke, come back to me son. Come back to me. Come back to me."

Tom's voice was constant. A metronome. Never-ending. Unchanging. Soon, it overwhelmed the chaos. Now, Zeke could hear Tom's voice cresting the wave of pain.

"Hold on son. Just hold on. What have I been telling you since you were little?"

Zeke's eyes were closed. He was on hands and knees in the alley, Tom laid on top of Zeke's back holding him as a young father holds his newborn son.

"Pain...is like...like a wave..." Zeke answered.

"...And that wave will eventually reach the shore..." Tom said.

Zeke felt the pain easing up...flowing away. His breath came easier.

"...and then...it's just a..."

The pain was almost gone.

"...memory..." Tom finished.

Tom let go of his son. Moved back. Concern on his weathered face.

"Better?"

"Yeah. Thanks Pops." Zeke stood on wobbly legs. Tom steadied him, supported his weight.

"Close call. I'm driving you home. No argument." Tom said.

"I don't have a choice, do I?" Zeke asked.

Tom smiled. "Nope."

Tom grabbed hold of Zeke's waist and they walked back through the alley, turned left, and went the back way to the pharmacy. At the street end of the alley, one of Mathias's men watched them walking away.

Chapter 6

Siodmak University, Thursday – Oct 10th

Like universities or community colleges all across the nation, students and faculty here hurried to or from their respective classes. The campus was a beehive of activity. Everyone industrious and performing their tasks with efficiency and diligence. The college, while small with an enrollment which hovered around ten thousand students, was modeled after the large universities in the Northeast. Majestic brick buildings, adorned with a center piece clock tower, fanned out in an eight-building quadrant which housed administration, the student hall and living dormitories, science and technology buildings (which were expanding), the theatre and liberal arts building, and an extensive food court.

All this, contained by manicured squares of fresh cut, uniformed pods of grass that students were forbidden to walk or sit on. But, students did anyway and the administration turned a blind eye as long as they didn't litter. Siodmak University also had a small law school filled with students competing for top honors.

The heart and soul of the university was the liberal arts curriculum. It was a dying breed of university, dedicated to making students think about the world through critical eyes while embracing their artistic, unique selves. This is why Val Rubin taught at Siodmak. She loved the breadth of academic freedom and diversity favored by the administration and her peers. The school was funded by an endowment that negated the need for corporate funds, donors, or rising tuition costs passed to the students. Here, if you wanted to learn, and had the aptitude, it didn't matter where you came from, or how much money your parents made. This university was open to all.

Val loved this university and felt privileged to teach and learn here. That was the real thrill. Learning from the students as much as she taught them. Maybe even more.

"Happy Birthday Professor V!" One of the students shouted.

Sixty years old! What the heck? I almost forgot!

Where did that time go Val wondered? She was happy, but it seemed like time was a thief that smiled in your face, then stole behind your back when you turned away. It stole your health...your dreams...your vitality. Time stole everything. But, time wasn't all bad. Time gave you perspective...wisdom...temperance...patience. Time was able to teach you many things, such as the best roads to take during rush hour, or just how far to hike before the sun set. It also gave mature women an edge younger woman didn't have yet. This thought amused Val as she watched her students sitting down for class.

"Thanks Meredith! Alright! Everyone comfy? I know this is Thursday and I don't usually start new sections until Mondays, but I was so thrilled about this topic that I HAD to start early! How many of you have ever heard of the term *Lycanthropy*?"

"Isn't that a band?" Meredith asked. The other students laughed.

"No, but it's a great name for one huh? Anyone else?" She laughed too. Val loved this class and her graduate students. This course, *Folklore, Mythology, and Urban Legends* was one she taught every Fall semester. This section about *Lycanthropy* had served as the precursor for her specific courses: *Werewolves Among Us: Shapeshifters, Myths, and Legends*, and *Lycanthropy: To Howl, or Not to Howl.*

Val had enough material from her research and courses to complete the book she was working on. Her hope, and plan, was to complete it next year, publish, then maybe retire to write fulltime. That is, if she got off her duff and wrote more than one page a week. At this rate, it would take Val three years to finish. That was doctoral thesis rate, and there was no way Val wanted to repeat that process.

Some of her students wanted to specialize in this obscure, but growing field, which pleased Val. Others liked the way it sounded and figured it was an easy "A". Either way, it didn't matter. She loved discussing mythology and the fictional creatures which lurked within our legends and superstitions.

"It's like werewolves, right? Like in those eighties movies?" Another student volunteered.

"Exactly! Ding! Ding! Lycanthropy is the condition of a person who truly believes they are, or can transform into a savage beast. These individuals often exhibit actual symptoms such as hairy palms and a thirst for human flesh." Val said.

"No shit? Oh! Sorry!" A male student said. He blushed as soon as the words escaped him. Others laughed. Val encouraged a judgement-free, safe zone in her class. Students could say and talk about anything they wanted. As long as they were respectful to her and each other. It made for lively debate and discussion.

"No, it's okay! When I first started doing research into this fascinating subject I said *No Shit* alot too! I still have lots of *No Shit* moments, which is part of the fun! Here...take a look."

Val started a Power Point presentation from her laptop. It displayed on a drop-down screen in the ceiling, in front of the main dry erase board. It was a painting of a large, wolf-like beast with black hair and protruding fangs. The beast seemed to stare out at the students with hunger in its eyes. It seemed hungry for their flesh. There was a feminine quality to the animal that was present, but easy to dismiss if not studied too close.

"Meet the *Beast of Le Gevaudan*. This beast terrified the residents of a tiny, remote town nestled in the mountain region of southern France. Over the course of three years hundreds of villagers were killed and mauled by some savage animal. There were multiple eyewitness accounts and even hunting parties tasked with capturing it. The years of 1765, 1766, and 1767 were called the "time of death" in the mountains. King Louis IX even sent a detachment of soldiers to hunt the beast because the killings could not be stopped."

"What happened?" A student asked.

"Eventually the beast was killed by a silver musket bullet blessed by a priest. I also found unofficial documents from the priest's protegee which indicated that not one, but several creatures like this roamed the countryside before they were hunted down and eradicated from the region. This was hard to verify, but it provides an interesting side note to this event." Val answered. She paused for dramatic effect. The students were enthralled. "Images and folkloric tales from all over the world share many similarities. Even as far back as the 1300s we have fantastic tales of werewolves and shape-shifters."

Val changed the slide. This time it was a wolf-beast, standing on two legs like a man.

Meredith raised her hand.

"Yes Meredith?"

"Do you believe Dr. V? That werewolves are real?"

Val pondered this.

"I...believe...there are many things unknown to us in this world. Some we will never know no matter how much research and searching we do."

"But do you?" Meredith pressed.

"I want to believe. How about that? Alright. Next slide..."

Chapter 7

Tom plunged a needle into Zeke's arm. "Ouch! Damn Pops! It's a good thing you're not a doctor!" Zeke said as Tom pushed the liquid through the syringe, took a small swath of cloth to dab the blood when he withdrew the needle, and tossed it in the sharp objects box on the wall.

"Don't be such a baby son. Got all those muscles but one little pin prick sends you runnin'!"

"Mom would've been gentle."

Tom nodded his agreement. "Yes, she would have been. That's a fact. Hopefully, this will help a little until we can figure out a more permanent fix. Speaking of which...I came across this professor lady up at Siodmak University...Professor Valerie Rubin. She might be able to help."

Zeke put his flannel shirt back on over his undershirt. He frowned.

"How Pops? We can't trust anyone with this."

Tom eyed his son. "You been sleeping?"

"Still have the nightmares. Maybe this will help with that too." Zeke glanced at his watch. "I've got to help Mrs. Ellis."

"I think you need to rest up son. She can wait."

"I promised her I'd help move that fridge off her back porch. What kind of man would I be if I didn't honor my word? I'm going to take the four-wheeler over there. See you tonight."

"Alright son. See you tonight." Tom said. He watched his son walk out and over to the small shed where he parked the four-wheel All-Terrain Vehicle (ATV).

"Yeah...what kind of man indeed." Tom said with a smile.

I love that boy.

Zeke lifted the three-hundred-pound fridge off Mrs. Ellis' back porch like it was a sack of flour. It was one of those rectangular ice boxes that people stored meat in. This one was old and rusted. The coils corroded and hardened so much that it wouldn't freeze anything. Zeke set it next to a tree by the unpaved driveway. Mrs. Ellis came out her front door and waved from the porch.

"I'll have Bobby and Jim from the dump pick it up tomorrow. At least you don't have to walk around it anymore." Zeke said.

"Oh, thank you Zeke! Tell your Father to call me! Anytime!"

Zeke nodded and waved. He climbed on the ATV and rode off whistling to himself. It was a bright, sunny day. Just over the treetops Zeke had a view of the mountains rising high into the Minnesota sky. He smiled. God surely smiled down on this place when he made it Zeke thought. He rode several miles, taking the long way back to his cabin so he could enjoy the fresh air. As he rounded a bend in the road he was surprised to find several vehicles blocking his way. Motorcycles. The group from the diner. Mathias was standing out front, holding his hand out like a police officer stopping traffic. Zeke stopped several yards away. He eyed the group. He was outnumbered ten to one. Zeke cursed himself for not bringing his rifle with him. Mathias smiled.

"Seems you are a busy man!"

"Mind moving your bikes? I've got errands to run." Zeke said.

Mathias waved him over. "Come on...Zeke...May I call you Zeke?"

Zeke stepped off the ATV but kept a careful distance. Mathias walked a few steps closer.

"What do you want?" Zeke asked.

"You...or actually...to ask you to work for me. No one has EVER done that to Blackie. Impressive."

Zeke glanced around the group and saw Blackie sitting on his bike glaring at him. Zeke nodded at him.

"I have a job."

Mathias laughed. The sound like screeching in Zeke's ears.

"Really? Bagging groceries at the shop-mart, or lifting boxes for old ladies? No...I mean fulltime work. Good paying work."

"No offense Mr..."

"Jones. Mathias Jones at your service."

"...Mathias...but I don't like you. I don't like him...And I don't like your troop or group or whatever the hell you call yourselves. I also don't like a bunch of wannabe badasses giving the folks of my town a hard time."

Mathias laughed again, further grating on Zeke's nerves. Zeke felt the hairs on his body stiffening and his breathing getting worse.

"YOUR town? Why this is America son! Home of the free! This is everyone's town! I was going to offer you a chance to run with us. Be an enforcer for my group."

Zeke stalked over to Mathias, crowding his personal space.

"Move or I'll move you." Zeke growled.

"And this is why I want you to work for me! Last chance. Yes or no?"

Zeke stared at Mathias, frowned, then spun away to walk back to his ATV.

"Cest la vie." WHAM! Mathias cracked Zeke over the head with a small club he was hiding behind his back. Zeke tumbled to the ground, landing on one knee. Mathias hit Zeke two more times. Zeke fell to the pavement, then the rest of the group joined in, stomping and kicking Zeke. They fell on him like a pack of wild animals. Zeke tried to defend himself, but the barrage was too powerful. He laid in the fetal position as Mathias' crew pummeled him. Blood poured from Zeke's mouth and nose. Mathias bent down, cupped Zeke's face in his hands, and stared into his eyes. The smile replaced by a dead-eyed gaze.

"I have to say...I REALLY don't like being told no. So, here's what I'm going do. I'm not going to kill you, but you will remember this little meeting. Then, I am going back into your lovely town and do whatever I want. If I see you in town again I WILL kill you...Now, it's time to talk to your old man!"

Zeke clawed at Mathias, but fell sideways. Blackie walked over and stared down at him.

"Not so damn tough now." He kicked Zeke in the face. Lights out. Zeke drifted off into the darkness...

Chapter 8

Pain. Agonizing pain. The pain was a throbbing, pulsing, living thing, pushing out of him. Zeke clawed his way toward consciousness with only his will to guide him. Zeke opened his eyes and found the Moon staring down on him in all its luminescence. It mocked him. Taunted him...

But, this time Zeke answered back.

Zeke's eyes bulged outward, the pupils darkening and turning yellow. The sockets widening and stretching as his skull shifted under his skin. Zeke's jawbone broke and elongated past what a human's normal shape would be. Zeke struggled for breath as his body morphed and changed. The skeletal structure cracked and reformed, lengthening and thickening until Zeke's body weighed three times more than before. As Zeke transformed he became aware of the sounds and smells of the forest. They invaded and overwhelmed his senses, flooding his nervous system with more information than his mind could process.

Heavy, matted fur erupted from his pores, climbing up and covering his entire body like vines in a jungle. Extra musculature grew underneath his skin, filling out and ripping his shirt and pants, until they hung in tatters, split at the seams. Zeke's body resembled that big green man from the 1970's TV show.

As the Moon illuminated the road in a huge swath of light what stood there was no longer Zeke...no longer a man.

It was something else.

It had the shape of a man and stood on two legs, but the arms were thick and heavy, the legs reformed to run faster than any human with short claws protruding from the animal toes. Long, sharp claws tipped his fingers as well. But, the head was the most shocking of all. Zeke's head retained some of the human shape, but his nose and mouth jutted out of a short snout like a wolf's and was filled with razor sharp teeth. Long, pointed, canine ears jutted from his head in place of his human ones.

Zeke was now...a *WEREWOLF*.

He stood in the middle of the road...panting. His breath visible in the cold night air. Even though he was an animal a core part of the Werewolf's brain knew and understood what he was. Deep inside Zeke was aware of events on a primal level. He also understood where he needed to go. To save the *FATHER*.

The Werewolf raced off into the trees, headed for Tarton's Mill...

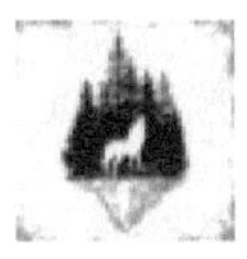

Night covered Tarton's Mill. The pharmacy was closed and all the lights off except for the back office where Tom squinted at the computer. He shook his head, trying to figure out how to input some figures. "Damn computers." He reached into a drawer and pulled out his reading glasses.

"Oh, that's better."

The sound of glass breaking came from the front room. Tom stood, walked to the doorway and found himself facing the barrel of a shotgun. It was Blackie. Mathias appeared from behind him, followed by a group of men.

"We need to chat good sir. Take a seat. You are about to become rich. I'm going to be your partner in this "operation", and in turn, you are going to supply me with all the opioids I need."

Mathias motioned to the small table in Tom's office. Tom sat. Mathias sat opposite him.

"So, I understand you are the big man around town. Kind of a home town hero. No matter! Here Mr. Atkins."

Mathias slid a piece of paper across the desk. Tom didn't touch it, but scanned it with his eyes.

"Morphine, codeine, oxycodone, fentanyl...you have it all. I need a new distribution hub since our last one was...Well, let's just say we had to beat a hasty retreat due to the aggressive law enforcement presence. But here you have no presence to speak of since your Sheriff's Department is spread out between this and three other small towns. As such, things here can be just as normal as always."

Tom studied Mathias. He'd seen men like this before. Arrogant and cruel. Holding a certain amount of sway over others, but inside a coward willing to do anything to seem all-powerful to his minions.

"Son. You don't scare me. I was scared during the war, and that's because there were a hundred-thousand Viet Cong troops trying to kill us. That was REAL fear son. But, a couple of low-life criminals who want to sell drugs to kids? No, you don't scare me at all. Actually, you make me laugh." Tom said.

Mathias hesitated. He expected fear from this older man, but was met with a courage he wasn't used to. Mathias was used to begging and pleading from his victims. False praise and deference. Mathias shifted in his seat. He tried to mask his nervousness.

"Oh Mr. Atkins, you are going to work with me, or we will do worse things to your boy that we already did."

Tom jumped up from the table, grabbed Mathias by the hair, and slammed his face downward, smashing it into the table with so much force that Mathias' nose cracked.

"Where's my son?"

Blackie and another man grabbed Tom's shoulders and yanked him down. Mathias held his head back so his nose would stop bleeding.

"Well done sir! Now that we have that behind us it is time to make you bleed! Blackie, your knife so that I may show this small town raffle some manners!"

Blackie gave Mathias his knife. Mathias admired the long, wicked blade and caressed it like a lover.

"Hold his arms down." Mathias said.

Chapter 9

Three of Mathias' men were posted in the alley next to the pharmacy. They smoked and laughed, telling each other dirty jokes about their girlfriends. The alley was pitch black except for one streetlight on their end.

From the far end the Werewolf watched them. He could see them with his enhanced night vision. He could see colors and patterns in the darkness that human eyes could not comprehend. The Werewolf tasted the night air. It brought back the sweet, pungent smell of the blood pumping through their veins and arteries. He listened for other sounds on the street. He heard the voices of folks in their houses and at the bar down the street. Engine noise from cars and trucks moving away from town reached his ears as well. The only humans in range were these wicked men. The Werewolf could smell the evil on them, glistening like sweat on skin.

These men...these sacks of meat wanted to hurt the Father. This thought filled the Werewolf with rage. His lips curled back from his teeth. He pawed at the ground, preparing to lunge forward.

"Hey. You hear that? Sounds like...I don't know...growling. Is there a dog down there?" One man asked. His partner shrugged.

"All I know is it's cold out here and everyone else is inside. How come we got this duty? Man! I need to take a leak too!"

"Sssh! You hear that now?" The first man said. He walked deeper into the alley...just out of the arc of light. He saw movement in the dark. Maybe two or three yards away. He pulled a small Glock from behind his back.

"Come out! Come out doggie!"

The Werewolf came charging out of the shadows at him. The man had no time to react as the Werewolf raked him across the chest with its sharp claws, tearing open his stomach, exposing his ribcage. The man attempted to scream, but the sound was cut short when the Werewolf tore his head off with one powerful stroke. The head went flying, landing at the other man's feet.

He screamed as he stared down at his buddy's head, the lips still moving. The Werewolf stepped into the light. At eight feet it towered over him like a grizzly bear standing on its hind legs. Its yellow eyes glared at him with the fury of a rabid animal. It threw back its head and roared into the night.

The man remembered the gun in his hand and pulled the trigger. Two rounds hit the Werewolf in the chest.

It growled.

They were painful, but not life-threatening.

It grabbed the man by the head and slammed him against the pharmacy wall, breaking his back, neck, and liquifying his internal organs. The man slid down the wall in a bloody, broken heap. It glanced around, located the fuse box on the wall. The Werewolf walked over and ripped the box off the wall. A low growl of satisfaction filled its throat. The Werewolf stalked back toward the end of the alley to the rear of the pharmacy.

The pharmacy was plunged into darkness. Mathias' men scrambled around trying to orient themselves inside a building they had never been inside before. Tom sat still. Mathias pointed at two of his men.

"Flashlights! You two...Watch him! Blackie with me!"

The two guards stared at each other. They whispered and kept glancing at the door and windows. Gunfire and shouting erupted from outside. Tom thought it sounded like the chaos of war. For a few seconds he was transported back to the rice paddies and jungles of South Vietnam. Another burst of gunfire rang out, causing Tom to flinch. He cursed himself in silence for this. He had been around enough gunfire to get used to it, but of course you never really got used to it. The men hunkered down below the window sills, trying to make themselves small targets in case someone fired inside at them.

"You two should run...now...Before it's too late."

"Shut up, you old bastard!" One of them said. Tom gave them a grim smile. He knew death was coming for them. And it didn't wait too long...More screams...this time inside the store.

One of the guards ventured into the darkness to check on the situation. Mistake. A big, hairy hand snatched him off the ground. Tom heard a crash as his body slammed into the shelves in the other room. The remaining man shivered as fear coursed through his body. He back away from the door as he heard heavy footsteps coming their direction. He used his gun and shot into the dark room.

Tom stood. He waited.

"What the hell is that?" He asked.

The Werewolf stalked into the room.

It glared at the evil human. The Werewolf wanted to rend the human to pieces. It turned its head and saw Tom staring back. The Werewolf's feral eyes softened.

The Father...Must protect the Father...

It let out a small howl as if acknowledging him. Then, it faced the guard with the gun. The guard fired point blank into the Werewolf's chest. The hits striking dead center. But, this did not stop death from coming for him. The Werewolf grabbed the guard by the throat, yanked him off his feet, and ran from the room. The guard's terrified screams were cut short, replaced by a tremendous howl which reverberated throughout the pharmacy. Tom slumped to the floor into a sitting position. He laid his head on his knees.

"Lord...please help us. Help my boy."

Chapter 10

Tom knocked on the door to Zeke's cabin. Silence. He knocked again. Tom lifted a small potted plant sitting near the stairs. A key was taped to the underside. Tom pulled it off and unlocked the door. It was dark inside. The air stuffy as if windows hadn't been opened in days.

"Zeke? Son? You alright?"

Part of him thought he should have brought a weapon. But, then he thought *why*? He wasn't about to shoot his own son no matter what. After talking to the County Sheriff about Mathias and his group, Tom had searched all over for Zeke. He'd followed the trail of footsteps into the forest until stopping at a stream he knew. Zeke must be have leapt over it. Considering the width, that was quite a leap. Tom needed to keep this in mind.

Tom pushed open the bedroom door. It was empty. The bed made but untouched. Then Tom heard sound coming from the bathroom. He tiptoed over, eased the door open, and peeked inside. Zeke was slumped against the tub shivering. His shirt was gone, pants shredded, his bare feet caked and covered in mud. His body was one giant bruise it seemed. Zeke was covered in welts and scratches from running through the underbrush and low-hanging branches striking him.

"Here." Tom grabbed a blanket from the top of the clothes hamper. He laid it over Zeke's shoulders.

"Are they...are they all dead...?" Zeke whispered.

Tom sat down next to his son. "Most of 'em. Not all."

"I didn't want to kill them Pops. I just wanted...I just wanted to make them go away...But IT wanted them dead. You know what I mean?"

"I do son. Either way, it worked. The rest of them cleared out in a hurry. Left their dead behind. Somehow, I don't think they'll be back.

At least no time soon. I spoke to the County Sheriff about it. He didn't know what to make of it. He had a run in with that group a few towns over, so he was not too sympathetic to their situation if you take my meaning. I didn't even have to lie since I was in that room the whole time. Store's a bit of a mess though. Gonna have to rebuild some shelves and do lots of cleaning."

Zeke's eyes were red. He'd been crying.

"I didn't want to do it!"

"Son...you were protecting me...Sure it's horrible and all, but I've known men like that, and they hurt other folks without a thought or care in the world. Listen to me son. You can't help who and what you are. I don't know if this is a curse or a blessing, but what I DO know is that you are special! And I'm not going to let anybody do harm to you. I love you. You know that right?"

Zeke nodded, but Tom wasn't sure if it was because Zeke was willing to accept this, or because of the shivers.

"If you are cornered don't think about it...you fight...you fight for your life. Understand?"

"I do Pops."

"Now. I'm going up to see that lady professor up to the university. If she can help us good. If not, we'll figure something else out. No arguments son. You stay here and rest till I get back. Maybe call Lila. She can help care for you." Tom said.

"I don't want her involved..."

"I'll tell her you had an accident. Don't worry. She's good people. Rest. Eat. I'll be back as soon as I can."

"Okay."

Tom stood. "I love you."

Zeke stared up at him. Fear and sadness in his eyes. It tore at Tom's heart to see his son this way.

"Love you too Pops."

Tom walked out so he wouldn't stay.

Chapter 11

Alexandria, VA. - Black Site, Friday – October 11th

Hammad and Steph finished packing the last of their equipment into the van. It was an ordinary, grey panel van, with the sign *ODESSA TOOL SUPPLIES* painted on the sides. They wore white, baggy uniforms that hid their tactical uniforms underneath. Loren stepped outside the house and joined them.

"Ma'am. Everything's packed and loaded. When we arrive at Andrews they'll get our gear stowed away and secured. They are prepped and waiting for our coordinates to the target location." Steph said. Loren nodded.

"Boss, we have something interesting." Hammad said. "Been tracking law enforcement chatter all week. A strange event popped up in Minnesota. A gang of criminals were attacked by some kind of wild animal. Pretty horrific details. No sign of it afterward."

"What's the town?" Steph asked.

Hammad continued. "Place called Tarton's Mill. What's weird is that the town doesn't exist. At least not on the maps. I checked deed and property records and there was a Tarton's Mill listed from 1930 until 1977. Then, it just vanished off all the maps. Sounds like it could be a good lead, but…"

Loren interrupted him. "That's it. Our guy's there. Any intel on the gang that was attacked?"

Hammad nodded. "Small time meth dealers. Outfit's run by a guy named Mathias. Real whacko. His people are mostly bikers that were kicked out of their MCs, stragglers, vandals, etc. No real loyalty except for the core group. Second-in-command's name is Blackie Delfini. Ex-con. Long record, blah, blah, blah."

"Find this Blackie. I want to talk to him. Both of you call your contacts and see if they can run him to ground." Loren said.

"Copy that Boss." Hammad said. They climbed in the van. Loren took one last look around before climbing in after them. She smiled.

The hunt is on.

Val's graduate students walked from the classroom as Val gathered her things. Tom walked up to the door and knocked.

"Hi! Uh...Professor Rubin?"

Val looked up and smiled. *What a handsome man!* "Yes! I'm Val Rubin. Come in. what can I do for you?"

Tom walked in. He shifted from foot to foot like a kid.

"It's been a long time since I've been out in the Big World. Guess I'm used to small-town life. Anyway, I was wondering if I could buy you a cup of coffee and bend your ear? I have a...well ma'am I need to ask you some questions about the subjects you teach."

Interesting. "You picked a great time Mr...?"

Tom walked over and extended his hand. "Sorry! My manners went all to hell. Sorry again! Tom Atkins. I've come up from Tarton's Mill."

"That's quite the drive! As I was saying, you picked the perfect time because my last class just finished, and I am done for the day. There is a lovely little coffee shop here on campus. Just a few buildings away if you want to walk."

"Sounds great Doc...uh...Professor Rubin."

She smiled. "Call me Val. Or Doc if that makes you comfortable."

Tom smiled. *Darn. She sure is pretty.* "Ok Doc."

Val and Tom to a relaxed walk to the campus coffee shop which sat right near the open-air quad. They sat at a small table facing the bulk of the campus.

"This reminds me of sitting on my porch staring out at the open sky and hills." Tom said. He smiled to himself as if remembering better times. Val watched him.

"Sound like a beautiful place...so tell me Tom...May I call you Tom?"

"If I can call you Doc." Tom said.

"What do you want to ask me about Tom? Are you familiar with the courses I teach here?"

Tom sipped his coffee.

"Mythology. Topics surrounding urban folklore and legends. Specialized graduate courses in Lycanthropy. That about right?"

Val was impressed. She smiled again. "Very Good Tom. Top marks for you!" When she saw his confused expression Val chuckled. "I lived in England for a few years studying at Oxford. I guess some of their colloquialisms rubbed off on me! But, yes. Before we go any further, what do you do? Retired military?"

"You're good Doc. Yes Retired. Fought in Vietnam. Lead an Infantry unit. Now, I run a small pharmacy. Kind of a pop without the mom operation. I figured helping folks was better than killing folks."

"Agreed. Thank you for your service though Tom."

"Someone had to go. I had family that served in World War II. They kinda passed that military trait down to me I guess."

"Did your wife pass away?"

"Yeah...died a few winters back...ok...more like ten, but it feels like yesterday. But it worked out alright. I met my boy and we've been doing good for the most part."

"You have a son. That's nice. I never got around to having kids...always wanted to."

"Actually, me and Valerie never had any either. My boy Zeke, I adopted him. But...he's my heart and soul. Been with me since he was five. He's grown now. Turned into a real good man. Makes me proud."

"So why did you come see me Tom?"

"What do you know about werewolves Doc?"

"I guess just what I teach. That they have some basis in reality, borne out of folklore, mythology, legends. Are you asking me if I believe in werewolves?"

Tom shifted in his seat, drank more coffee before answering. "I'm guess that's what I believe."

"I want to believe. But sometimes, our beliefs and our realties clash." Val said.

Tom stared into Val's eyes. His gaze direct and unflinching.

"I believe Doc."

The words hung there. Val started to laugh, but swallowed the motion when she realized Tom was not laughing. The gentleness in his eyes, and pleasant demeanor he'd displayed since walking into her classroom was gone. Replaced by a hardened man who seen and experienced horrors she could never understand. No matter what Val believed, what Tom believed was as concrete to him as the chairs they sat on, or the Earth under their feet.

"You're serious?"

"Doc, I'm a veteran of two wars...was a cop for about ten years. I believe in what I can see...other than God I guess. I feel kind of silly, but what I'm saying is that I need your help Doc."

Val pushed her cup away. She leaned forward, intrigued and mystified by whatever Tom was going to say. "Help with what?"

"It's better if you see for yourself. Can you come up to Tarton's Mill? Just for a day or so? I want you to meet my son Zeke. I know you don't know me, but I was thinking...well...I was wondering if you wanted to drive down with me? It's a couple hour drive. And to be honest I could use the company."

Val was trying to process all that Tom said. To him, it seemed like his intentions might be unseemly. Tom coughed into his hand and smoothed his thinning hair back. "We do have a lovely bed and breakfast in town. I know the owner. She wouldn't charge you anything to stay. I mean...if you wanted to that is."

Val stared at this man in front of her. He seemed sincere and kind of sad. She felt safe near him. He had a protective quality to him that gave her tremendous confidence. The sadness he exuded made Val want to hug him.

What a strange thought.

Val had never driven off with a strange man before, but her gut told her it was okay. Besides, she had her zap stick in her purse.

"I'd love to." Val said. "My schedule, like every weekend, is open. Sounds fun!"

Tom stared into his coffee cup, as if expecting to find buried treasure. "I didn't want you to think I was some kind of pervert."

Val laughed. "Never crossed my mind. On the way you can tell me about your wife." The mention of his Valerie made Tom smile. He was starting to like Doc Rubin.

Chapter 12

Joint Base Andrews, Prince George's County, Maryland

Friday – October 11th 10:02am

Loren rubbed the spot on her inner thigh where the cuts were. She could not see them, but felt them through the fabric of her tac pants. He pressed fingers against them, willing pain to come forward. The pain was good. It was her friend. It made her remember...

Frank tried to speak, but his throat was a ruin. She could see the ground underneath and his life fluid leaking away. She cradled him in her arms, trying to keep him from dying. He lifted a finger to her face, traced the outlines, then stopped breathing. His eyes staring sightless into the void from which there was no return. Loren heard gunfire and shouts. She turned, still holding her dead husband, and saw HIM. The boy stood at the farthest edge of the compound. Staring at HER.

The boy was only ten, but as large as any man and twice as strong. She also saw the defiance on his face. The rage. Happy that her Frank was dead. The boy ran to the compound wall, jumped up ten feet, caught the edge, and disappeared over the top. The sirens and alarms continued to ring, but Loren knew they wouldn't find him. Not tonight. Not soon. But...SHE would find him. Even if it took till the end of her life.

The C-17 aircraft rocked from side to side as it rode the slip stream. The motion comforting to Loren as she joined the present again. Loren called Hammad and Steph over. "Is the team meeting us like I asked?"

"Yes ma'am. We rendezvous here." Hammad pointed at his GPS device. "Then we convoy to the staging point right outside Tarton's Mill."

"Good." She said. Loren unbuckled and they walked over to several long black boxes secured to the deck. She punched a code into the top of one and a small panel slid open. She reached inside, pulled a latch and the side of the box slid aside with the hiss of compressed air. She pulled out a smaller box and opened it. Inside were bullets, color-coded with red and blue tips.

"Are they...?" Steph asked.

"Silver? Yes. Intel suggests that regular lead bullets will not bring him down. Silver is supposed to be lethal." Loren said.

Hammad frowned. A rare gesture of emotion from him. He trusted the Boss, but something felt off. "I thought our mission was to capture?"

"That's still the mission. These blue bullets are more like rubber riot control bullets. They should stun him enough for us to bag him and tag him. The small amount of silver nitrate should work as a sedative." She said.

Hammad picked up one of the red bullets. "And these?"

Loren gave him a small smile. "I call them the Eliminators...Weapon of last resort." She stared at the men. Handpicked from thousands of candidates. Loren trusted them. "This has to go smooth. We will be working in a town full of civilians. Collateral damage should be kept to a minimum. But, if anyone gets in our way they are to be considered enemy combatants. I want to take him outside the town if possible."

Both men nodded their understanding. They knew what was required of them. This was their job, and they were good at it. Steph handed Loren a folder. Inside, photos of Tom and his pharmacy. "Tom Atkins...seventy-two...owns the only pharmacy in town. Lives alone...his wife died ten years ago." Steph said.

Loren paged through the folder.

"Ten years huh? Any children?"

"None on record." Steph said. "We have local intel that says he is close to young man. Calls him his "son". Guy does odd jobs around town. Stays low. Keeps to himself mostly. By all accounts people seem to like him."

Loren looked up. "What do we have on the son? Anything?"

Steph shook his head *no*. "Nothing. No prints...no driver's license...No bills in his name...no parking tickets. Guy's a ghost. Name is Zeke. And here's the kicker. This guy has been living in the town for ten years."

"That's our boy." Loren said.

Zeke felt better. Tom was right. His body was healing faster and faster every day. The beast inside him was strong, and its blood made sure Zeke was strong too.

Today was the first day he could feel the Werewolf inside him during the day. Aware of him, and he, of it. He could feel it yearning to be released. To run. To hunt. To prey on those that preyed on the weak. The immuno-suppressants Tom gave him kept the Werewolf at bay...For now though. It would have its time. Zeke was sure of it. The Werewolf was dangerous. But, not to everyone.

As Zeke thought more about it he realized that he felt no compunction to attack the residents of Tarton's Mill. In fact, all his instincts felt protective of them, and of this place. This town and territory belonged to him; and the Werewolf.

And they would defend it to the death.

Zeke felt so good that he decided to go down to the pharmacy on the ATV and clean up. He drove to town and parked around back. When he shut the engine off his eyes were drawn to the alley. Zeke compelled himself to walk closer. Zeke saw reddish-brown stains covered the ground. Zeke stood near them, staring down, transfixed. His mind filled with horrifying sounds and images.

Screams...

Blood...

Howling...

Guilt seized him. He knew those men deserved what they got, but the thought of having killed people filled him with nausea. But, that primal part of his brain where the Werewolf lived was glad. Even now, through the guilt, Zeke was glad too. And the fact that he was glad sickened him.

"Zeke? Hey!"

Zeke turned when he realized someone was speaking to him. It was Lila. She placed a soft hand on his shoulder. "You okay Zeke?"

"Yeah."

"It's pretty awful huh? Just like Johnny Gamble...the pedophile. Wonder what did this?"

Zeke shuddered. "Someone horrible."

She faced him. "Don't you mean "something"? There is no way a person did this. Ripped them apart? No...it was definitely an animal. My money's on a bear. You remember how we had that grizzly come down two summers ago? It killed two people as I remember."

"Scar...yeah...I remember." Zeke said. And he did.

When Zeke came back to town, after the dark times, he hiked into the woods. Back to the old spots where he used to adventure as a young boy. It wasn't long before he ran into Scar. The old bear sat among the ruins of two hunters. They had tried to kill him for sport, but the bear got the hunters first. Zeke entered the area quiet, in a non-threatening way. He respected Scar and didn't want to hurt him.

But, this time the old bear didn't recognize Zeke. It charged him. Hurtling toward Zeke with all his might, ready to savage this human interloper. Zeke didn't have time for conscious thought. The Werewolf took over. It killed Scar. When Zeke returned to consciousness he found himself sitting on the ground with Scar a few feet away...his throat torn out.

Zeke cried out to the heavens as he mourned the old warrior...

"You know what's weird?" The question shook Zeke from his revelry. "Now I remember, the hunting party found the grizzly dead a few days later. Looked like another predator killed it. Must have been another bear I guess."

"Guess so." Zeke mumbled.

Lila noticed Zeke was quiet. She felt this place of death disturbing him.

"Hey. Wanna go somewhere? Let's get out of town for a while."

Zeke looked into her eyes. "Ok."

Chapter 13

When they pulled up to the cemetery in Lila's battered old Toyota Zeke thought they were stopping to stretch their legs. They had been driving for an hour, northwest of Tarton's Mill. The cemetery must have been a hundred years old or more. It sat on a big hill, facing mountains to the east, and a deep valley to the west. The plots situated on a series of gentle rolling hills which sloped down to a lazy river below. For a cemetery, it was a tranquil place. Zeke felt a sense of solitude as they walked between and around the headstones and grave markers. Zeke noted dates as old as 1901.

Being here, in this place, reminded him of a moment in time with Tom that changed both their lives.

Lila pulled a bottle from her small backpack and took a long swig. She closed her eyes as the liquor washed false warmth down her insides. "Here." Lila passed Zeke the small bottle of whiskey. He glanced around the empty grounds.

"You sure we should be drinking here? It feels disrespectful." Zeke said.

"Lots of cultures celebrate their dead by bringing them food and drink. So, think of this as a celebration!"

"Uh, okay. Whose grave is this?" Zeke sipped from the bottle. Lila had stopped in front of a headstone. Zeke passed the bottle back to Lila. She smiled down and took a drink.

"My Dad's. He's been gone a little over twelve years now. He was a gentle man. Always treated me like a princess...today's his birthday. I miss you Daddy."

"What about your Mom? Is she alive?" Jake asked.

"Yeah. She lives in Canada. Don't see her much. We don't get along to well. Better off apart I guess.

Zeke didn't answer.

"You ever feel like an orphan Zeke? I know you have your Dad and all...but I mean more like...out of place? Like you have a secret and there's nobody in the world you can tell the secret too? You know what I mean?"

"Sometimes."

Lila sat down and laid back on the grass. She stared up at the bright blue sky. Zeke laid down next to her.

"I want to be more than a waitress. Not that I have anything against being a waitress. It's just that I stuck around to help my Daddy with the house and when he died I just never moved on. Never did anything worth doing. God! I'm babbling, aren't I?"

"It's okay. I like your voice. It's calming."

Lila touched Zeke's face. She traced the contours and outlines with a finger. "There's something about you. Something on the edges...you have an aura around you different than everybody else. Daddy said I came from a family of gypsies or something and that the women in the family all had what they called "second sight"

"So, you're some kind of physic?"

Lila sipped from the bottle and passed it to Zeke. He drank. He was starting to feel the effect of the liquor.

"Sometimes...not often...I get a feeling that something's going to happen. Or, I can feel negative energy or positive energy coming off people in waves...Like those men in the diner. They had a dangerous energy. It covered them like a dirty blanket. But your Dad for instance...He's got this light coming off him that makes me want to dance in it!" She said.

"I know what you mean. When I'm around my Pops it feels like...like..."

"Everything's going to be okay..." Lila finished.

He smiled at Lila. She leaned over and kissed Zeke. "Was that okay?"

"It was nice." Zeke said. "So, do you get a feeling with me?"

"Something's blocking me...It's like you're an open book on one hand...and on the other...Can't see it right now. Like I said...you're different. Here..." Lila reached into her shirt and pulled out a chain with a cross on it. She took it off and placed it around Zeke's neck.

"I can't take this Lila."

Lila placed her hand on top of his.

"It's a gift. I was taught that you give where your love goes." They stared at each other for a long time. Neither one speaking. They kissed again. This time long and slow. When they pulled back from each other they stayed connected. Their noses touching. *I could stay here forever*, Zeke thought.

Lila sprang to her feet. She pulled Zeke up with her. "Come on!"

Zeke was wobbly from the whiskey. "Where are we going?"

"Your place." Lila said. She ran back up the hill, pulling Zeke along behind her.

Chapter 14

50 Miles South of Tarton's Mill, Friday – October 11th, 2:00pm

Loren and team sat inside a small storage unit, located behind a non-descript office park fifty miles away from Tarton's Mill. The room was lit by one flood light set in the corner. It cast a bright gaze on a man seated at a table. He wore a black hood over his head, and was zip-tied to the arms and legs of the metal chair. Loren sat opposite the man, staring at him like a predator. She nodded at Steph who jerked the hood off. The man blinked his eyes. The floodlight blinding him. He could just make out three shapes in the room with him. He stared with unfocused eyes at Loren. Hammad and Steph wore black masks. Loren did not.

The man was Blackie.

"What the hell? Who are you?" He said.

"Tell me about the pharmacy."

Blackie stared at her like he hadn't heard the question. Loren nodded. Steph walked over and punched Blackie in the side of the head. The chair toppled sideways, slamming to the ground. Blackie cried out. Hammad and Steph picked the chair up.

"What happened? What attacked your gang?"

"Look, you crazy bitch...I don't have to tell you shit!" He spit across the table. The gob of saliva reached her end, but not her. She stared down at it and nodded again. Steph hit Blackie in the back of the head this time.

"Stop...please..."

Loren leaned forward. "I thought ex-cons were tough. I guess you're not so tough without your crew huh? Have you seen this man before?" She showed him a photograph of Tom. Blackie nodded.

"Okay. So, tell me about what happened."

"We ah...we went in to roust him. Get him to be our supplier so we could run meth in the town. Then some kind of animal attacked us. It was BIG! Like a wolf, or a bear, or I don't know! Some kind of monster! It killed a bunch of our guys. So Mathias and I, and some others booked. We took off. He told us to go different directions so the cops couldn't track us all! That's it! That's all I know!"

Loren nodded. "Did you see another man with the pharmacist? Young. Named Zeke?"

"Yeah! That Sonafabitch! Got all cocky and shit! So, we lit into him good. Left him out on the road. He won't be talking shit anymore I can tell you that! So...we good? That's all I know."

"Thank you Blackie. You can go now."

Blackie glanced around. "Really? You're cutting me loose?" Steph and Hammad stepped backward and off to the side.

"Yes." Loren pulled her gun and shot Blackie through the forehead. His brains exploded out the back of his skull, splattering the wall behind him.

"Let's go. Torch this place." She said.

"Copy that Boss." Hammad said.

4:15pm

Loren watched the town of Tarton's Mill through a pair of binoculars. She could see people milling around. They looked like ants from here. Loren liked that. Ants that she would squash if she had to without a moment's hesitation. Steph walked up. "Alpha Team just arrived. Bravo is standing by on the east side of the town."

"Good. Let's go over the Op plan."

Steph signaled Alpha Team. They were battle-hardened men and women. Former Military. Contractors. A few mercenaries. They were all flinty-eyed and squared away. Loren gave them a cursory nod before laying out a large map on top of a long black gear box.

"This map shows the layout of the town and surrounding properties. My guess is that he lives outside town, but close enough to go in to shop, eat, etc. I want two-person squads to insert here and here. Bravo will ensure general containment. My team will search the outlying properties and if we come up short we'll converge on the town...Steph?"

"We are hunting a predator. I just want to be clear on this. Do NOT take him for granted. Even if he has not changed you need to treat him as such. Blue-tips should incapacitate him enough for us to collar and restrain him. Our team will be the only one with terminate authority. Keyword to execute is FERAL." Steph said. He handed out blue ammunition boxes to the team. "I'm lead tracker, so be sure to follow my instructions."

Loren stared at every team member. Her eyes flinty. Their faces were grim. They were ready. Steph had assembled a good team.

"Thanks Steph. Remember...we are hunting the most dangerous animal on the planet. Treat him as such. Let's go to work."

Chapter 15

Tom drove slow and steady up the highway toward Tarton's Mill. Val sat next to him, staring out the window. They had stopped for a bite. Afterward, they drove for forty-five minutes lost in their own thoughts. But, it wasn't uncomfortable. In fact, the more Tom thought about, the more he noted that it felt natural. Like they had taken road trips like this hundreds of times.

"Is this weird Tom?" Val asked.

"What's that?"

"How natural this feels? We've just met each other, and traveling like this...I don't know. It feels comfortable. It's so very hard to describe."

Tom glanced over at Val and smiled.

"I was just thinking the same thing Doc."

"You were talking about your wife before. She taught high school?"

"Yep. She was over-qualified I'd say. Had a PhD in History."

"Really? And she never wanted to teach at the University level?"

"Nope. Not her thing. She liked to say, "I want to keep my ear to the ground, and the best way to do that is to stay connected to the youth of our country. For the life of me, I don't know why she was with an old dog like me. One of life's mysteries I guess."

"Seems like she was one smart women." Val said.

"Smarter than me by a long shot."

"Can I ask you a question Doc?"

"Sure."

"How come you aren't married? I mean...well...it's just that you are a beautiful woman and...I mean. Oh darn! I should have led with intelligent huh?" Tom laughed. Val joined him.

"I'm not too up on gender politics these days. I meant it as a compliment."

"And I took it as one Tom. No worries. I was married for many years. It was not a good time. He was an alcoholic. A mean one...You know I consider myself a smart, tough woman, but sometimes your heart doesn't allow you to do the right thing...or weakness...or...I don't know. I stayed longer than I should have."

"Sorry I pressed you Doc. Really."

"It's okay."

Tom and Val rode in silence for a time. He was mad at himself, and thought maybe he'd asked too many questions.

"But, the divorce pushed me to take stock of my life...figure out what I wanted for a change and go after it." Val said.

"Good for you. I mean it."

"You say things straight from the heart don't you Tom?"

"It's the only way to be right? I believe in being straight with folks. The same way I want folks to be straight with me. That's how I live my life."

"Tell me about your son Zeke."

Tom's face lit up. He smiled.

"That boy saved my life..."

Tom told Val about how deep into misery he was after Valerie died.

The day of the funeral he stayed by the gravesite, unwilling to move. Tom sat by her grave until everyone, including the cemetery workers left. He pulled a bottle of vodka from his inside pocket, opened it, and drank half the bottle in two great gulps. Tom stood and staggered over to a huge tree with an umbrella of branches which blotted out the afternoon sun. Tom pulled another object from his pocket...a small revolver. It was loaded.

Tom stared at the gun. Hefted the weight. Checked the chamber. He cocked the hammer and stared down the dark barrel. And he waited...

Tom was close to pulling the trigger when he saw movement in a thicket of bushes near the tree he was leaning against. He stood, walked over to the bushes thinking it was a dog. Tom bent over and parted the bushes. What he saw shocked him out of his depression. A young boy sat shivering inside the bushes, half naked and terrified. "Hey there...it's alright. I'm not going to hurt you. What're you doing out here by yourself?" Tom asked.

The boy stared at Tom with vacant eyes. Then, he did something surprising. The boy leaped up and wrapped his arms around Tom. Hugging Tom so tight it almost cut off his air. "Whoa! I gotcha...I gotcha."

Tom hugged the boy back, and then it happened...

Val stared at Tom for several minutes. Tom took a deep breath before continuing.

"What happened?" Val asked.

"I fell in love for the second time in my life. Took the boy home and we raised him together until Valerie passed. Never even thought twice about it. It just seemed...It was right and good. Zeke's my son and that's that."

"You're a good man Tom." Val said. Tom didn't answer. He just smiled and kept driving. Val pretended to look out the window as they continued along the highway, but most of the time, she watched Tom.

Tom parked the truck in front of the pharmacy. He and Val got out and went inside. Everything on the street seemed normal, except the dark van parked a few blocks from the pharmacy. Inside two Alpha Team members watched Tom. The passenger spoke into a portable radio.

"Positive ID on the pharmacist."

Loren's voice crackled over the radio's speaker. "Copy that. Keep eyes on him. We'll pick up the ball once he crosses the town limits."

"Copy that."

Alpha Team van crew waited until Tom backed away from the pharmacy and pulled back onto the street, headed out of town.

Chapter 16

Lila glided through Zeke's house. Her hands caressing Zeke's furniture, the appliances, the paintings, portraits of he and Tom. As she did, Zeke watched her. She looked like an angel. Delicate, yet strong. Ephemeral and mysterious. Lila felt Zeke watching her. She turned and smiled at him. She noticed a small box on the table. It was labeled to Tom. It was open and several vials were visible. The vials were labeled: *immuno-suppressants*. She picked one up, staring at the fluid contents inside.

"What are these?"

"Uh...medicine. I have a...condition...Nothing contagious. Kinda like an auto-immune disease."

Lila nods. She leaves the box and wanders over to the bedroom door. "My dad had something like that too. He was always in a lot of pain. Do you have pain Zeke?"

"Yeah, I do."

"Aren't you lonely living up here all by yourself?" She asked.

"Nah. My Dad's up here alot. We have dinner together...drink a few beers and watch sports. You know, just hang out. Guess I've been alone most of my life. Kinda used to it by now. I'm not always so good around other people...It's just better this way."

Lila stares at Zeke. A look of extreme concentration on her face. "See. There it is again. Something inside you...Something dark and hidden. What are you hiding Zeke? You can tell me."

"I can't tell you this. I'm sorry. Maybe we should go back to town so I can get my ATV."

"No. I'm sorry. I didn't mean to make you uncomfortable."

"You don't make me uncomfortable Lila."

"Come here." She said.

Zeke stumbled over. He felt like a zombie. His legs wooden. She took his face in her hands and stared into his eyes.

"You're trembling."

"I'm nervous." He said.

Lila kissed his eyes. Then his forehead. Then his lips. She placed her lips on his ear.

"Is this your first time?" Lila whispered.

Zeke nodded. "I've never been with...my life's been pretty tough. You know?"

"I do...I do Zeke."

Lila led them to his bedroom. She laid a hand on his chest, motioning him to sit on the bed. As Zeke lowered himself down Lila began to take her clothes off. The afternoon sun cascaded through the windows, illuminating her in a golden glow. Her hair seemed to shimmer and dance in the light.

"You're...so beautiful..." Zeke said.

Lila helped Zeke out of his clothes and they pulled the covers back on the bed. Zeke rolled over on top of Lila.

"Lila...I'm not...who you think I am..."

"I don't care." She said. She pulled Zeke down and into her.

They made love...It was tender and loving. Zeke felt as if his soul had always belonged to Lila. Their bodies moving in perfect rhythm. Cresting each wave until they met in the same place. Zeke wrapped his arms around Lila and held her.

"I think I love you Zeke Atkins. I know that's crazy, and you don't have to say it back, but I do."

Now, Lila felt vulnerable and exposed. Zeke pulled her closer.

"I love you too Lila. Crazy or not."

Lila smiled. Minutes later she drifted off into a dreamland filled with monsters and shadow shapes. Zeke watched her sleep.

What am I doing?

Zeke was aware of someone in the house. He sprang up like a feral animal. Alert and ready to fight. He edged toward the door, all his senses alive. Before he heard Tom's voice, Zeke smelled his father. He relaxed and walked back to the bed to wake Lila.

"Hey Lila. My Pops is here. Get dressed." Zeke whispered. He kissed her cheek, then got dressed. Zeke knew someone was with his father. He smelled Val's scent as well. Lila murmured in her sleep. Zeke smiled and decided to give her a few more minutes. He eased out of the bedroom. Zeke and Tom smiled at each other. Tom crossed the small room in a few strides and hugged his son.

"Damn Pops! You were only gone half the day!" Tom pulled back, a little embarrassed. He guided Val forward by the elbow.

"This is Doc...err...Professor Val Rubin. From Siodmak University."

"Hi Zeke!"

Zeke shook the offered hand, but kept his distance. He still wasn't sure how this university professor could help them.

"You too ma'am. Pops, can I speak to you alone for a minute?"

"Be right back Doc. Have a seat anywhere."

Val stood off to the side like an intruder.

"Lila's in the bedroom." Zeke said. Tom stared at his son for a minute, not comprehending what Zeke said.

"Lila? She's...? OH! I got it son!"

Tom and Zeke tried to hold their laughter, but it didn't work. Soon, both men were ripping out belly laughs that descended into snorts. Val smiled as she watched them. The love and affection between the two, obvious and genuine.

"Ma'am. Sorry about my manners. Would you like to have supper with us? My friend Lila's going to join us too." Zeke shot a glance at Tom, who grinned.

"Are you sure? I feel like I'm intruding."

"No trouble at all Doc. Any special dietary restrictions? We're meat eaters in this house." Zeke and Tom both stopped for a sec, after Tom said it. Before the pause got too awkward, Lila floated through the doorway, over to Tom, and hugged him like family.

"Hi Mr. Atkins! I missed you!"

"I missed you too Lila. Hey. This here is Doc Rubin from the university."

Lila faced Val, smiled and walked over. She gave Val a huge hug also. Val was surprised, but didn't resist.

Lila pulled back but took hold of Val's hands.

"Oh...she's pretty Mr. Atkins! And...kind too."

Val shifted from foot to foot. "Thank you Lila."

Lila had a faraway look in her eyes. Like she was staring at a distant landscape, somewhere the others couldn't see or go. Lila shook her head and stared into Val's eyes.

"You can trust her. Well, what are going to eat? I am famished!" Lila danced over to Zeke.

Chapter 17

Hammad, Loren, and Steph crouched in the trees several meters from the house. They spoke in hushed whispers.

"The target is inside, along with three civilians." Hammad said.

"We need to separate him from the others in order to get a clear shot." Steph added.

Loren nodded. "Understood. I think in this situation I should approach him. Ask him to surrender to us."

Both men stared at her, surprised. "Uh, Ma'am. That's not procedure." Hammad said. "Rules of engagement clearly state that..."

"I understand the rules. Please don't lecture me on them again. Understood Sergeant?" Loren said to Hammad. Her icy stare made him look away. Hammad was embarrassed. He'd never questioned Loren's authority before.

"Yes Ma'am. Understood."

Loren began unstrapping her holster when a rumbling noise made her pause. She and the others looked in the direction of the noise and saw a group of motorcycles coming up the lane to Zeke's house.

"Who're these guys?" Steph asked.

Loren didn't answer him. Instead, she spoke into her throat mic. "All teams...be advised we have potential combatants in our sector. Standby to engage but do not come in unless I call...click to acknowledge."

Several radio clicks came back in response.

The group rode up and parked in front of the house. The leader was Mathias. He stepped off his bike, waited for the rest to do the same. He glanced around like a conquering general and smiled.

"ZEKE ATKINS! Come out and face me!"

Inside, Tom and Zeke looked at each other. They were all mid-bite into their meal. Val was confused. Lila, silent. Tom stood, walked to the small front closet and pulled out a shotgun, tossed it to Zeke. Tom pulled a rifle out, checked the chamber, and glanced out the window near him.

Tom scowled. "Mathias. That sumbitch. Ladies, if you would be so kind as to lay on the floor under the table." Tom said.

"Uh...Tom...What's going on?" Val asked. Her eyes darted back and forth. Violence of any kind was foreign to her. Lila took Val's hand and guided her to the floor. They crawled under the table.

"Sorry Doc. We had a run-in with some trouble makers a few days ago. Guess they came back looking to end it."

"I'm waiting!" Mathias shouted from outside.

Zeke opened the door.

"Wait! I feel darkness. Don't go outside...please" Lila said.

He smiled at her.

"It's okay Lila. Be right back."

Author's Note:

This is a book about Fathers and Sons. Being a father is my mission in life and I love my sons with all my heart. I will support you and help you become the men I know you are (and can be)! This book is dedicated to my sons: Trevor, Pablo, Elijah and Gavin.

And...as always...to my Susie. Thank you for always believing. I love you.

Additional Note: *Siodmak University* is a fictional university set in the fictional town of *Cold Water*. As is the town of *Tarton's Mill*.

Other Books by Kevin L. Williams:
  HUNTED
  The Guardians: Baltimore, 1862
  Re-Animated Love, Book 1: Awakening